D1189010

Tom and Pippo's Day

PIPPO

HELEN OXENBURY

WALKER BOOKS
LONDON

When I wake up early in the morning, first I give Pippo a hug.

Then we go to see if Mummy
and Daddy are awake.

Daddy has to
hurry with
his breakfast.
Sometimes I give Pippo some of mine, but he's so clumsy and he makes a mess.

Pippo and I do
things together all day,
until Daddy comes home.

When it's bedtime, I sometimes don't know where Pippo is and I have to look everywhere until I find him.

Because when it's time
to go to sleep,
I need to be
with Pippo.